1:26.9

# Top Gear

BBC Children's Books
Published by the Penguin Group
Penguin Books Ltd, 80 Strand, London, WC2R 0RL, England
Penguin Group (Australia) Ltd, 250 Camberwell Road, Camberwell, Victoria
3124, Australia (a division of Pearson Australia Group Pty Ltd)
Canada, India, New Zealand, South Africa

Published by BBC Children's Books, 2011
Text and design © Children's Character Books, 2011

Written by Rac Newman and Sam Philip

# TopGear

# Contents

# Hello and Welcome!

## Annual Report

### Name

Jeremy Clarkson

### Good times

- Zoomed round a proper NASCAR track in a Mercedes SLS AMG
- Tested the Ferrari 458 Italia, and found it to be rather brilliant
- Met Cameron Diaz and got three hugs
- Raced the sun across Britain – and won

### Bad times

- Knackered the Mercedes' tyres and waited ages to replace them. Twice
- Drove the deeply disappointing Bentley Mulsanne in Albania
- Wore chauffeur's trousers made of black sticky tape

### Overall mark: B+

## Annual Report

### Name

James May

### Good times

- Got to look at lovely old aeroplanes in Albania
- Drove up an active volcano – and survived
- Successfully cleared a Norwegian road with the *Top Gear* snow-bine
- Drove faster than the others in the Bugatti Veyron Super Sport
- Played golf in a proper astronaut suit

### Bad times

- Got knocked out in the desert
- Got very cold in promotional clothing at a German racetrack
- Had to do yoga on American TV

### Overall mark: A–

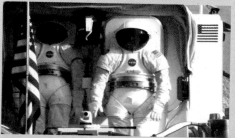

# Annual Report

## Name

Richard Hammond

### Good times

- Drove the best car in an Old Testament NASCAR race
- Finally found a car that was faster than something else in a race – the VW Touareg Dakkar
- Got to drive lots of Porsches, including a 997 GT3 RS

### Bad times

- Built a rubbish motorhome that was flimsy and cold
- Got lost in New York, which he thought was a scary place
- Had to listen to Genesis, turned up very loud, in Turkey
- Lost his wedding ring in Norway

### Overall mark: B

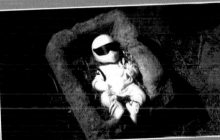

# Annual Report

## Name

The Stig

### Good times

- Born in a stable; got gold, frankincense and a games console as gifts
- Clinched a victory over the Aussies in a rally race (oh, no, that was 'James')
- Set a new lap record in the Ariel Atom V8

### Bad times

- Set an even faster lap record in the Pagani Zonda R, but it didn't count
- Got blown up, rammed a truck, went swimming in a carwash
- Failed to get round the track in a Reliant Robin
- Had to wear James' stripy sweater

### Overall mark: 1.08.01

# WHEN BRITAIN WAS GREAT

In 1913, there were 140 carmakers in Britain. What went wrong? The producers reckon it's that classic British sports cars were rubbish, which was why everyone dumped them for foreign hot hatches. Could Jeremy, James and Richard convince them that Britain was ever a great sports car maker?

*Right-ho, chaps. Your mission: buy a classic British sportscar for under £5,000, meet at the old Lotus factory, and prepare to undertake a series of challenges.*

Jeremy was tempted by a car from his youth. He got a 1974 Jensen-Healey; James got a TVR S2 from 1989; and Richard also had a gem from his younger days – an egg-yellow 1994 Lotus Elan SE. It was made of plastic, like the TVR, which is obviously better. Lighter, anyway.

## Challenge 1: Speed

*Race round the Lotus test track, to see which of your ridiculous cars is 'best'. Then the Stig will set a much better time in a Peugeot 205 GTI.*

Jeremy loved the sound of his Jensen's engine, but the gearbox didn't sound so good. Richard struggled to defend his car's front-wheel drive. James praised a little-known safety feature of the TVR: the delay between pressing the accelerator and the engine doing anything. 'The car says, are you sure? Oh, alright then.'

So, the laptimes. **Lotus:** 2.09.0min, **TVR:** 2.15.9, **Jensen-Healey:** 2.17.9.  For the Stig's lap, Jeremy couldn't find a Peugeot 205 GTI, so Stiggy did it in a diesel. Same difference. But he could only manage 2.22.0 – **a win for the Brits!**

## Challenge 2: Reliability

*Drive from Lotus (now owned by the Malaysians) to the grave of TVR in Blackpool, via the remains of the Jensen factory in the West Midlands.*

This is a journey of 280 miles. The Stig was to follow them in a well-made, practical Vauxhall Astra GSi. Sadly, he had a bit of a problem and… blew up a little bit. No harm done, luckily.

Bits fell off Richard's car, but he felt it was just shedding weight to make itself more efficient. And the window that didn't shut meant he got a refreshing breeze (and quite a bit of rain). Jeremy found his rock-hard seats meant it was sensible to stop often, which was nice.

> We've done **20 miles** so far, which is about 7, 800km. After a distance like **that**, your back is going to hurt a **bit.**

> It's not that we don't make sports cars anymore. We don't make **anything**.

## Challenge 5: Practicality

*Load up a Golf GTi with garden centre goodies, then see how much you can fit in your cars in comparison.*

The Golf GTi proved deeply impractical – it couldn't even get one metal rose arch in. Jeremy managed a bamboo and a conifer. Richard fitted a giant urn and a naked lady statue. James did even better: 'TVR – a car that came out of a shed, now underneath one.' A final **win** for the British sports car. The Great British sports car. Why on earth did we stop buying and driving them?

## Challenge 3: Safety

*Get dragged into the side of a lorry at 50mph.*

The Stig went first, in a Citroen AX 3. His car got a bit mashed up, but he was fine. Then Jeremy had a go. He was a bit nervous. Result: **another win for the British sports cars.**

> Seat belt is on. Good, **strong** dependable seat belt – oh, I'm off! **Bye!**

## Challenge 4: Waterproofness

*Take your cars through a carwash.*

The TVR passed with flying colours, as did the Jensen. 'Nuclear submarines have more leaks than this does.' Richard was a bit wet afterwards, but he had an explanation.

> Nobody these days is saying, ooh I'd **love** an old XR3. But a Jensen-Healey, a TVR, a Lotus? **Yes!**

**KRUMP!**

> No, it's fine. I spilled my drink. Just as it started. Just water, and a bit of soap.

> There are, of course, good reasons why so many of these **great** names have gone. But after our journey across the width of Britain, we **couldn't remember** what they were.*

Then the Stig took a Ford Escort XR3i through, and also got a bit wet. **Yet another win for the Brits.**

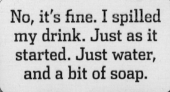

*Let's be honest – it had something to do with reliability, safety, comfort, speed, price, handling, practicality…*

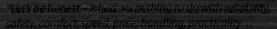

9

# The Many Moods of James May

The highly technical *Top Gear* Mood-o-meter can give an accurate measurement of the feelings of the presenters. First up: James.

**Very Happy**

**Happy**

**What?**

**Slightly Miffed**

**Pretty Grumpy**

You ate a **chocolate bar** in my car.

**Livid**

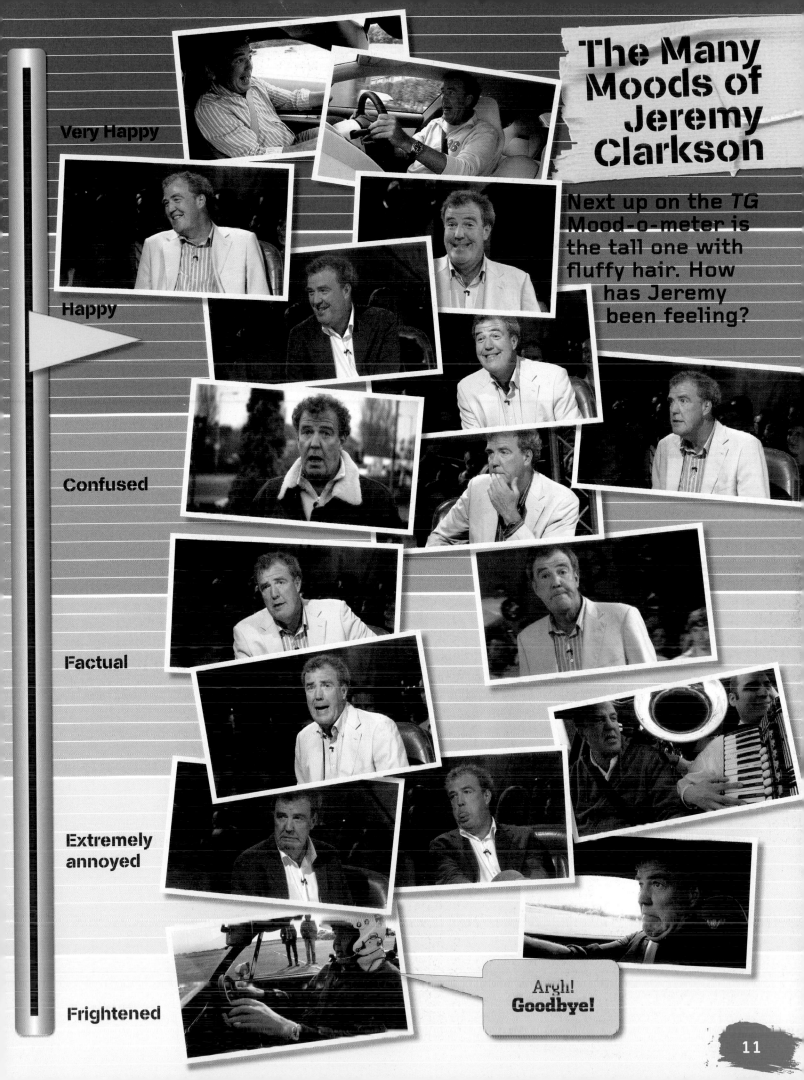

# The Many Moods of Jeremy Clarkson

Next up on the *TG* Mood-o-meter is the tall one with fluffy hair. How has Jeremy been feeling?

**Very Happy**

**Happy**

**Confused**

**Factual**

**Extremely annoyed**

Argh!
**Goodbye!**

**Frightened**

11

# The Many Moods of Richard Hammond

The most excitable presenter almost broke the Mood-o-meter. Richard can get dangerously worked up over a simple news story.

**Bonkers**

**Manic**

**Excited**

**Happy**

**Frightened**

DAMN.

**Crushed**

12

# The Many Moods of Stig

This was a tricky one for the Mood-o-meter. Could it detect any measurable emotion in the tame racing driver? What do you think?

# Match the Simile

A simile is a phrase comparing different things, to show that they are in some way alike. Jeremy loves a simile. Every car he drives is apparently like something else entirely (quite often, dogs or gods). But can you match these cars with their simile?

**Bentley Continental Supersports**

It sounds like squirrels are being pushed into the engine.

Listen to that noise! It's like Barry White eating wasps.

This car can be vicious, but in an amusing way, like a shark in a funny hat.

It sounds like the god of thunder gargling with nails.

It's a bit like sliding down a black run in a wardrobe.

It sounds like a bear. Like a burning bear.

It stops like a duck on a frozen lake.

It looks like a dog doing a poo.

It's like driving a – fast! – bouncy castle!

This car is like an elephant with the reflexes of a water-boatman.

**Saab 9-5 Hot Aero**

**Chrysler Crossfire**

**Hummer H2**

**Prodrive P2**

**Overfinch Range Rover**

**Mercedes McLaren SLR**

**Pagani Zonda F**

**Ferrari 458**

**Mercedes-Benz CLS 55 AMG**

# Piste Bashing

Richard took on some hardcore snowmobilers in a chunky VW Touareg Dakkar. The race went down a mountain, and across a frozen lake. But who won?

**START**

Richard can use white or blue spaces, the snowmobilers can use white or red ones. Who needs the least number of spaces to get to the finish line?

**Come on!** Find grip!

**FINISH**

**This** is where the race is won or lost!

# CATCHPHRASE BINGO

You know what you're going to get with *Top Gear* – you can almost predict what Jeremy is going to say. You could even make a game out of it. A game like this.

| | | | |
|---|---|---|---|
| A series of challenges | Ambitious, but rubbish | It's time to put a star in our reasonably priced car | Good news! |
| Jezza | Please welcome our guest | And on that bombshell | Flappy-paddle gearbox |
| Let's do the news | Loser! Loooser! | Powerrrrrrr! | How hard can it be? |

| | | | |
|---|---|---|---|
| And across the line! | Let's do the news | How hard can it be? | All we know is, he's called... |
| How it does around our track | See you next week, take care | Captain Slow | On tonight's show |
| Ambitious, but rubbish | Back to the studio | Morris Marina | Twin-turbo |

| | | | |
|---|---|---|---|
| On tonight's show | And on that bombshell | Loser! Loooser! | Drag race |
| It sounds like... | How do you think you did? | And that means handing it over to our tame racing driver | Hamster |
| Now, we've got to move on | Coming up to Gambon! | How hard can it be? | Your time. Was. One minute. Forty... |

## How to Play

*Up to four people can play at once. Pick a card and cross off the phrases as you hear them. The first person to fill their card (or with the most crossed off) is the winner.*

| | | | |
|---|---|---|---|
| It sounds like... | Good news! | And across the line! | Some say... |
| Do you want to see the lap? | Back to the studio | Carbon-fibre | Supercar |
| A series of challenges | How do you think you did? | The producers said... | Aaaargh! No! |

17

# Motorhome Madness

**Look at it! It's enormous!**

**It's absolutely superb. Do you ever watch *Grand Designs*? Every single thing they do looks like this.**

Motorhomes are clearly much better than caravans. But they're all either American, comfy, and too big for our roads, or British, small and ugly. Surely the chaps could design something that was good to drive AND practical to sleep, cook and wee in?

**Aargh! Aargh! Oh my God! No, this is terrifying! I can't *begin* to explain what this feels like.**

## What they did

Richard went old-school: a Land Rover with stone (effect) walls. The loo was where the passenger seat used to be, with the loo roll mounted on the dashboard.

Jeremy went designer: a block of flats on top of an old Citroen. Arranged over three floors were a Japanese contemplation garden, a proper cooker with a grill, and two hammocks. And a conifer in a silver pot out front.

James went hardcore. He fitted a superlight space age metal pod on the roof of a Lotus. It didn't look very comfy.

neck when he got some speed up. And the fold-out walls weren't held on very well.

But the biggest clot was Jeremy, because the ridiculous high box made his Citroen wobble more than a jelly on a washing machine.

## Sleeping

James was ready in ten seconds. Jeremy was ready in ten seconds. Richard took many hours of sweating and swearing to fold out the carpets, conservatory, games room, dining room, library, spare room… until he gave up. That night, the strong winds made most of his roof fall off, and the walls squeaked and rattled non-stop.

**It's a roofbox with a sleeping bag in it. Where's your bog?**

**There.**

**Eww, where your head is!**

## Driving to Cornwall

James was perfectly happy driving his Lotus down to Cornwall. His roofpod weighed less than him, and made almost no difference to the handling. But he'd screwed a bit of wood over his petrol cap.

Richard had cut the back off the cab to fit his cottage on the Landy, which meant a stiff wind hit him in the

> **Look.**

However, Jeremy's block of flats proved to be even more useless.

## Putting on a wetsuit

The chaps were told to drive onto the beach and change into wetsuits to go surfing. Jeremy was fine. James had no room at all, and banged his head repeatedly.

Richard was able to leave all his motorhome behind to head to the beach, but this meant he had no sides on his Land Rover and

> Ow. Oww. **Oww!**

no privacy. He borrowed a child's tent instead.

The tide came in, and Richard and James left in a hurry without

getting changed. Jeremy took his time, and almost sank as a result.

## Cooking a meal

Despite not having the best ingredients, all the chaps did manage to cook something. Sadly, none of it was edible. And on this campsite, it was Richard that managed to set fire to his home.

> He's actually set fire to **metal**! How's he done **that?**

## Having a wee

This was possible. But not attractive. Richard could wave at passers by from his loo. And James was too hunched over to wipe his bottom with dignity.

## Better than caravans?

Overall, the camping holiday was not proving to be a brilliant success.

> I'm covered in **egg**, and **crisps**, and **Spam juice**. I haven't shaved or had a proper wash for three days.

And Jeremy's wobbly tower block was so slow that it held up more traffic than a caravan would. For a laugh, while he went for an ice cream, James and Richard decided to park it right on the edge of a cliff. But it fell off, and broke into a billion bits.

As usual, they'd failed. But in an **interesting** way.

> What's **that?**

# MotorChef

Camping should **never** mean you can't eat properly. Let our presenters show you how to make delicious food using only ingredients bought from a small rural garage, and cooked in their DIY motorhomes.

Right, what I'm going to cook tonight is Spam slices coated with a crushed cheesy popular snack item.

Do you have any steak?

No.

Pork?

No.

Er... Lamb?

No.

Bacon?

No, sold out. Sorry.

Do you have any... butter?

No.

Lard?

No.

Margarine?

**WARNING: Ask a responsible adult (not someone like Jeremy, James or Richard) to help you with the oven, should you actually want to cook anything, but we don't recommend any of this nonsense.**

# Starter

## Ingredients
- *1 tin of Spam*
- *1 bag of Quavers*
- *1 packet of Jaffa Cakes*
- *One egg*

## Method
1 Empty the Quavers into a mess tin and crush them lightly with a fork.
2 Slice the Spam into neat regular slices – about 1/8" or 2.5mm thick.
3 Crack the egg into a bowl and beat lightly.
4 Dip the slices of Spam in beaten egg, then Quaver crumbs, and fry gently.
5 Scoop the orangey bit out of half a dozen Jaffa Cakes into a pan.
6 Warm gently and pour over the Spam slices.
7 Serve immediately. Into a bin.

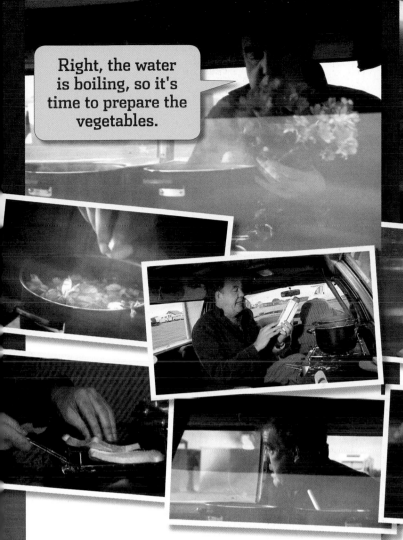

Right, the water is boiling, so it's time to prepare the vegetables.

What I propose for dessert is Eton Mess, crossed with trifle.

# Main course

## Ingredients
- 1 tin of corned beef
- 1 bunch of flowers
- 1 jar of pickled onions
- 1 bottle of oil (even if it's engine oil)
- 1 tin of sardines
- 2 slices of white bread

## Method
1 Boil a pan of water. Pull the heads off the flowers and drop them in the boiling water.
2 Add a couple of pickled onions for bite and flavour.
3 Look at the engine oil dubiously.
4 Throw the horrible flowers away and have sardines on toast instead.

# Dessert

## Ingredients
- 8 slices of white bread
- 1 large tub of natural yoghurt
- Assorted bars and bags of chocolate
- Assorted fruity sweets
- Assorted flavours of crisp
- 1 tin of squirty cream
- Butter
- 1 egg

## Method
1 Cut the bread into fingers and line a bowl with them, overlapping the pieces.
2 Pour the yoghurt into the bread-lined bowl. Leave to soak in.
3 Break up the chocolate into bite-sized pieces and add to the yoghurt.
4 Mix some butter and beaten egg, and heat gently over a low heat.
5 Somehow set fire to your motorhome, even though it's made of metal.
6 Have a liquid dinner instead as the sun sets, listening to the creak and crackle of your cooling motorhome.

# Trackday Cars Challenge

Times are tough. Not many people can afford to buy a car just for thrashing round a race track. So why not buy a normal four-door saloon that is also good to go racing in? The *Top Gear* chaps were given £5000 to investigate.

> Ah, **Belgium**. The mecca for the performance motorist.

> It's not the **first** place you think of going for a performance saloon car.

> If we **do** crash, this will take some explaining.

## The Cars

James: a Mercedes 190 Cosworth, that he was secretly confident about for technical reasons no one else understood. It also had first gear in a confusing place.

Richard: a BMW M3, the cheaper series 2, with a shocking toffee and caramel interior.

Jeremy: a twenty-one-year-old Ford Sierra Sapphire Cosworth. 2 litre, 16v. Unlike the other two (made in Germany), it was built in Belgium.

## Challenge 1: Speed

*German autobahns don't have speed limits, so earn 1 point for every mph over 130 you can manage.*

James struggled to pull away at the lights, as he kept putting his car into reverse instead of first gear. And the autobahns proved rather full of East German lorryists doing sensible things. All of the boys went much faster than they would have been allowed to in the UK.

> **Traffic**. Lot of trucks, lot of trucks.

## Challenge 2: Oompah

*To see how practical your cars are, carry some passengers for the next part of the journey.*

That sounded simple enough, but the passengers turned out to be four big men in leather shorts with massive musical instruments: accordion, trumpet, trombone and tuba – an oompah band!

Richard went deaf; Jeremy could only fit them in with the sunroof open and gave up very very quickly; James broke down.

The band preferred the BMW, because it was from Bavaria, like them. Jeremy wasn't happy.

## Challenge 3: Faults

*Your cars will now be tested for faults by a mobile ADAC patrol.*

A yellow truck folded, expanded and twiddled out into an amazingly hi-tech garage. Once he worked out how

> Paah! You're not serious? **Six?** You may as well have got nought.

to make it go forwards, the German tester discovered an awful lot wrong with James' Mercedes. It boiled over, the wheels were very wobbly, there was rust everywhere…

Jeremy's Sierra was in pretty good nick, but Richard's M3 appeared to have been badly bodged after an accident. A good score would have been 150; Jeremy got 58, James got 19, and Hammond got… 6. Out of 150! His car was officially judged dangerous.

## Challenge 4: Track lap

*Wearing promotional clothing from your vehicle manufacturer, take your car to the track for a fast lap driven by the Stig's German cousin. You have to sit in the passenger seat.*

James was very unhappy with his outfit. He started to go the same

> Holey moley! That's **not** a good look.

colour as his horrible T-shirt when Deutsche Stig thrashed the Merc round in 2m19.3s.

Jeremy was very enthusiastic about his car's racing heritage, and very frightened by how near Herr Stig got to a big concrete wall. He managed 2m14s.

Richard was very worried about his car's safety, but he did manage a lap of 2m6s.

> Wall. Wall. **WALL.**

## Challenge 5: YouTube

*Like all the proper race-day geeks, record a lap with a dashboard-mounted camera and post it online. One point for every hit you get on YouTube.*

James got lost quite quickly, and only got seventy-one viewers. Jeremy wasn't entirely honest about his speed, but managed 137 hits.

Richard was too scared to drive his car fast, so he pretended to break the camera so it only

> **120mph** in a car that only scored **6!**

recorded sound (actually just him making 'brum-brum' noises). As a result he ended up with only seven hits.

## Challenge 6: Economy

*With only three gallons of fuel, try and drive out of Germany.*

The nearest border was Poland. James was highly confident, as his car was meant to be much more efficient than the others. But in the end, Jeremy won (just), Richard came second and James ran out of fuel. At this point James was badly behind in the scores, and looked pretty glum.

> You just **lied** and then sped up the film!

> Hang on, I scored **minus** what I already had!

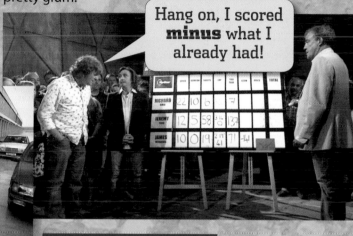

## Challenge 7: Price

*One point for every pound under £5000 your car cost.*

Richard paid £3990, so scored 1010 points. Jeremy paid £4999, so only got one point and was very annoyed. 'I may as well have bought a toy car!'

But James paid only £2990, so he scored 2010 points! He was the clear winner and did a little victory dance!

## What a result!

It's *Top Gear* official: the best everyday saloon that you can also use as a trackday car is a slow, rusty, wobbly-wheeled, small, uneconomical piece of junk.

> **Yes!** And on that bombshell, it's time to say **goodnight!**

# Ring It to Win It

The Nurburgring is where fast cars go to find out just how fast they are. It's also where Sabine Schmitz (in a van) tried to beat Jeremy's lap time (in a diesel). Recreate these epic battles in a much smaller, cheaper way.

Pagani Zonda R
6min 47sec

Ferrari 599XX
6min 58sec

## How to Play

- Cut out the playing pieces, fold as shown and glue. Or find something small, like coins or buttons, to use as playing pieces, if you don't want to cut up your book!
- Two or four people can play. Roll a dice to see who chooses their playing piece first.
- The Ferrari 599 XX and Pagani Zonda R can use the red or blue spaces. They can switch from the red to the blue lane whenever they cross a black line.

- Jeremy in a diesel can only use the red spaces, Sabine in the van can only use the blue spaces.
- Start from the yellow line, and 'drive' clockwise. Roll a dice to see how many spaces you move each turn. The Ferrari and Zonda can roll again every time they get a six.

25

# The Best Car I've Driven This Year

The chaps got to drive some rather nice cars in the last year. But which one was best? Let's look at the numbers!

## James in the Porsche Boxster Spyder

 Engine: 3.4 litre flat 6
 Power: 320bhp
 0-60mph: 5sec
Top speed: 166mph
Price: £46,000

### Pluses

- 80 kg lighter than the standard Boxster, thanks to aluminium doors, aluminium engine cover, superlight wheels and carbon fibre seats.
- Lots and lots of fun. 'I've owned a standard Boxster S for the last four years, and I can promise you this is better. It's revvier, it's more eager; it's excellent.'

### Minuses

- Absolutely no extras. No aircon – too heavy. The doorhandles are scraps of red cloth, and the plastic shield over the dials is missing.
- Costs £5K more than the standard Boxster, for less bits (see above).
- Putting on the tent roof – sorry, 'sun shield' – is a lot of fiddly effort. And then the top speed is reduced to 126mph – any faster, and the tent will blow away.

> I'm **fizzing** massively here. I'm fizzing fit to burst. Nurse!

> I just **love** muscle cars. I love the idea of taking an ordinary basic car and adding more and more and more and **more** power until it's just about unusable, and then you put it on sale.

## Richard in the Chevrolet Camaro SS

 Engine: 6.2 litre V8
 Power: 426hp
 0-60mph: 4.9sec
Top speed: 146mph
Price: £40,000

### Pluses

- It's a good-looking film star. You probably know this car as Bumblebee from *Transformers*.
- The chassis is from the Australian Vauxhall VXR8, which *Top Gear* loves.
- You get plenty for your money: 'Unlike other muscle cars, the suspension isn't made from lamp posts and logs.'

### Minuses

- Richard also drove the Mercedes-Benz E63 AMG, which sounded better. 'Listen to that! It's the AMG dawn chorus. When it comes to noise, the Benz blows the Camaro out of the water.'
- It's also faster and more powerful than the Camaro. But it does cost £72,000.
- Jeremy thinks the Camaro is only driven by stupid violent people.

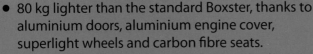

## Jeremy in the Ferrari 458 Italia

**Engine:** 4.5 litre V8
**Power:** 562bhp
**0-60mph:** 3.4sec
**Top speed:** 202mph
**Price:** £170,000

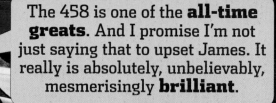

> The 458 is one of the **all-time greats**. And I promise I'm not just saying that to upset James. It really is absolutely, unbelievably, mesmerisingly **brilliant**.

### Pluses

- Jeremy thinks it's much better looking than the Ferrari F430... which James owns.
- It's faster than James' F430. Much faster. 'James' car is gone! It's just a humiliation!'
- Having James' car to race against gave Jeremy somewhere handy to eat chocolate and crisps.

### Minuses

- It has flappy paddles for the gearbox behind the wheel. But so as not to be confusing, all the other things that are normally operated with levers behind the wheel are done with buttons instead, mounted on the wheel.
- The satnav is in the same place as the speedo – so you can know where you are, OR how fast you're going, but not both. 'I have no idea how fast I'm going now. I just know I'm somewhere near Guildford.'

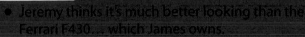

## James in the Bugatti Veyron Super Sport

**Engine:** 8.0 litre W16
**Power:** 1200bhp
**0-60mph:** 2.5sec, 0-100 in 4.5sec
**Top speed:** 267mph!
**Price:** £1,600,000. Sorry.

### Pluses

- It's still a comfortable proper car, with windscreen wipers and a CD player.
- It has a super-slippy surface to help it slide through the air as easily as possible. Which looks gorgeous.
- It can get to 100mph in the time a Porsche 911 GT3 needs to get to 60mph.

### Minuses

- The tyres cost £20,000 a set, and Bugatti has no idea how long they will last.
- At top speed it gobbles 7.7 litres of fuel and 45,000 litres of air every minute.
- Why does it need the added power of a Golf GTI just to do an extra 5mph? 'The reasons are quite complicated, and I've been barred by the producer from explaining them properly.'

> God speed Captain Slow! 258, 270 – I'm going faster than I can speak! It's **unbelievable**, look how fast everything's going past!

# How fast is 257mph?

James clocked a staggering 257mph in the Bugatti Veyron Super Sport on the test track. Here's what that means in real terms...

**KA-POWWW**

## 0.88 seconds
*to cover the length of a Premiership football pitch*

## 15.6 seconds
*to drive the length of the Top Gear test track's 1800-metre main runway*

## 2 hours 21 minutes
*to drive from Land's End to John O'Groats*

## 27 minutes
*to drive right the way round London's M25 ring road*

## 929 hours
*to drive from the Earth to the Moon*

## 97 hours
*to drive right the way around the Equator*

# SURF'S UP!

On their motorhome trip to Cornwall, the boys found surfing to be seriously tough. But this beachy wordsearch is so tricky that it makes surfing look like, erm, riding a bike!

It's the easiest thing I've **ever** done.

```
D U P S M I R O B E D I T H R O A X
E D A P O N I P D A R N H A N E B U
E N F L O C F L R L U D A W A V E S
W I S A N D N I A K N R C T G R A P
A Q O S W E T S U I T U K H G O C R
E N I H I F U T G C O B E O I M H I
  S I V O P I I A E U P L N S N A I T
  O G E F E T T M F T Y A D S E N S A
  P G S F O H R O I R T N E O R T I C
  P O T E U U O R L A H D L C S R T O
  A F I N T W A E A M O R L U U U J N
  Y S B A I R R X N E R O U W R W U D
  C O R N W A L L O Z I V S N F R R U
  N I A M O P E R R I F E L U B A C K
  M L C E Z A T E M O H R O T O M H L
  U E N R A N T T V E O U R O A J R A
  Y B U M X O S E E R Q N G P R E I W
    Y R O L S U T O L R D E G Y L D P M S
```

WETSUIT
WAVES
SURFBOARD
WIPEOUT
MOTORHOME
BEACH
SEAWEED
LIFEGUARD
LAND ROVER
CITROEN
LOTUS
CORNWALL
TIDE
SAND
SPLASH

# Three Wheels of Terror

Forget the North Pole. Forget the African desert, and the Bolivian jungle. This challenge is definitely the toughest journey Jeremy has ever made. And he has to do it... in a Reliant Robin. Will he make it?

> I've always been **worried** that this would have a profound effect on the handling.

## The Car

A basic car, stripped down to beyond the basics: it only has three wheels, and it's made from plastic. It was amazingly popular – the second best-selling plastic car in history. Reliant used more fibreglass than anyone in Europe in the '70s. But deciding to put the single wheel in the front may not have been the best idea in the world.

Luckily a balding popstar happened to be passing with his dog, and helped tip him back on the level. At the next left-hand turn, he dropped onto his right bumper **again**, but managed to flip back up by opening his door.

## The Route

Jeremy may have bitten off more than he can chew here. He has to drive from a garage on the outskirts of Sheffield… to a pigeon loft in Rotherham. That's almost fourteen miles! Fourteen miles of dangerous roundabouts, pedestrian crossings, pedestrians and traffic lights. Jeremy demanded a proper racing harness and a crash helmet before he even got into the Robin.

## The Journey

Jeremy gathered his courage, started the engine, set off down a gentle slope… and rolled over! **Disaster!** The big feller made it topple over to the right when he turned left.

KKRNTCH

Then he tried to apply 'Power!' to the 850cc engine, but only succeeded in flipping the front end up. So he couldn't steer, and **hit a lamp post**.

KKRNTCH

> Oh no, I've **crashed** it. I've crashed it almost **immediately**. I mean literally, twenty feet.

KKRNTCH

**I'm fifty years old. And I'm lying on my side, in the street. In Sheffield.**

**KkRNTCH**

**KkRNTCH**

The distant prospect of a top speed of 85mph proved too tempting, as well. So he **tipped over again**, well before getting anywhere near it.

Another aging celebrity helped Jeremy back on his way. At this point he decided to ask some Robin fans for advice… after **rolling it AGAIN**. They suggested a bag of cement or a big toolbox on the passenger seat, to help balance it out. And only going in straight lines.

After eight miles, enough was enough. He headed for a garage to try and sort out the stability problems, but drove straight into the inspection pit. (Single wheel at the front, Jeremy. Remember?) Using memories of his first bicycle, he got the chaps to add stabilizers.

These six-inch rubber wheels bolted on to the battered plastic sides of the Robin gave Jeremy vast amounts of undeserved confidence. And then guess what…

**KkRNtcH**

**BBC LOOK NORTH**

He didn't listen, to be honest. He **turned it twice** in the background of a live news report, but luckily the reporter sorted him out. Then he ended up on his roof in the middle of a cricket pitch.

**KkRNTCH**

**SPLASH**

**With my new anti-capsize solution in place, I knew nothing could go wrong. And I knew that right up until the moment when it did.**

# MIXED-UP F1 DRIVERS

They're some of the fastest men on the planet, but can you recognise these top Formula One drivers with their helmets off? To give you a hint, we've jumbled up their names. It's your job to unscramble them before the race starts!

## SPIES A FLAME
_ _ _ _ _ _   _ _ _ _ _ _

## KERB BE WARM
_ _ _ _ _   _ _ _ _ _ _

## JUST NO BONNET
_ _ _ _ _ _   _ _ _ _ _ _

## VALIANT BEE TESTS
_ _ _ _ _ _ _ _ _   _ _ _ _ _ _

## SUCH A CLICHE HAMMER
_ _ _ _ _ _ _   _ _ _ _ _ _ _ _ _

## NOON AND LOAFERS
_ _ _ _ _ _ _ _ _   _ _ _ _ _ _

## SAW THE MILLION
_ _ _ _ _   _ _ _ _ _ _ _

# LOOKS LIKE RAIN!

"Oh no! I need to erect the top tent!"

As James discovered, the Porsche Boxster Spyder is a very bad car if you're caught by a sudden downpour. But where does it rank on *Top Gear's* Ten Worst Cars In The Rain?

**Porsche Boxster Spyder** You'd need to be a professor of astrophysics just to understand how the Boxster Spyder's roof works. Unfortunately, James isn't a professor of astrophysics. He got wet.

**Richard's MG TF limousine** A giant sports-car-limo might be the coolest way to arrive at a glamorous awards ceremony, but you'd best pack a raincoat if the weather forecast looks bad!

**Bugatti Veyron Grand Sport** The convertible Veyron doesn't have a roof. It has… an umbrella. But it also has over 1000bhp, which is surely enough power to blow the clouds straight back where they came from…

***Top Gear's* convertible Espace** The boys' attempt to build a convertible people carrier didn't go well. As they soon discovered, the cabrio-Espace wasn't resistant to water. Or monkeys.

## McLaren-Mercedes SLR Stirling Moss
Only seventy-five of these amazing roofless speedsters were ever built, each costing £600,000. An expensive job to repair the seats when they get ruined by rain!

**Ariel Atom** Jeremy's favourite face-bending car doesn't have a roof. In fact, it doesn't even have a windscreen! If it starts to rain, you'll just have to outrun the storm…

## Citroen C3 Pluriel
The Pluriel's roof is one of the most complicated in history. Once you've taken it down, your only chance of staying dry is driving the C3 straight into a garage… and leaving it there!

**Maserati GranCabrio** It's one of the most beautiful big convertibles ever built, but watch out for rain clouds: the GranCabrio's big roof takes a full twenty-eight seconds to close!

**Morgan SuperSports** The roof of the SuperSports is simply two big sheets of metal that must be bolted into place by hand. Best bring along a friend if you're planning a drive on a cloudy day!

**Citroen 2CV cabriolet** You wouldn't have much chance of outpacing the rain in the creaky old 2CV. Even with the roof up, it was so leaky that you'd still get soaked in a downpour!

TG ♥ USA

Rain
Seattle
**Washington**
Olympia
Vancouver
Portland
Salem
**Oregon**

Snow
**North Dakota**
Bismark ● ● Fargo

**South Dakota**
Pierre ●

**Montana**
Helena ●

**Idaho**
● Boise

Cowboys and nothing

**Wyoming**
Cheyenne ●

**Nebraska**
Lincoln ●

**Testing muscle cars**

Nice flat bit for going fast
● Bonneville
● Salt Lake City

**Nevada**
Reno ●
Sacramento ●  ● Carson City
San Francisco ●

**Utah**

● Denver
**Colorado**

Topeka
**Kansas**

Las Vegas ●

**California**

Desert

Santa Fe ●
Flagstaff ●
Albuquerque ●

Is this the way to ● Amarillo ?

Oklahoma City ●
**Oklahoma**

● Los Angeles

**Arizona**
● Phoenix

**New Mexico**
Aliens

● Tucson

Dallas ●

**Playing with Ken Block**

El Paso ●
Chilli

**Texas**

Austin ●
Houston ●
Oil

Jeremy, Richard and James can't get enough of the United States, so they keep going back. Here's a reminder of where they've been on their holidays.

CT = Connecticut
DE = Delaware
MA = Massachusetts
MD = Maryland
NH = New Hampshire
NJ = New Jersey
RI = Rhode Island
VT = Vermont
● = state capital
● = city you may have heard of

Minnesota

Michigan

Minneapolis
St Paul

Wisconsin

Milwaukee

Madison

Iowa

Michigan

Lansing

Detroit

Used to make cars here

Chicago

Des Moines

Cleveland

Pennsylvania

Ohio

Pittsburgh

Harrisburg

Illinois

Indiana

Columbus

Philadelphia

Springfield

Indianapolis

Cincinnati

Louisville

Frankfort

West Virginia

Washington

Baltimore

Dover

Annapolis

DE

MD

Amish

Jefferson City

Missouri

Kentucky

Charleston

Virginia

Richmond

Montpelier

VT

NH

Portland

New York

Concord

Albany

Boston

MA

Providence

Hartford

CT

RI

NJ

New York

Trenton

Maine

Augusta

Country music

Nashville

NASCAR

Raleigh

North Carolina

Arkansas

Tennessee

Memphis

Little Rock

Birmingham

Columbia

South Carolina

Mississippi

Alabama

Atlanta

Georgia

Charleston

Louisiana

Jackson

Montgomery

Baton Rouge

New Orleans

Tallahassee

Hicks with rocks

Orlando

Florida

Stig's American cousin

Miami

**Going for a nice drive**

**Buying a car cheaper than a rental one**

# The Ingredients of a Muscle Car

Richard loves them, but how exactly do you make a muscle car? Follow our handy step-by-step recipe and you'll be cooking up a noisy, smoky feast in minutes!

**ENGINE:** Must be large and powerful – ideally a huge V8 with none of them fancy turbochargers or superchargers. With muscle car engines, bigger is always better. Anything smaller than a five-litre engine and you'll be laughed out of the muscle car club.

**COUNTRY OF ORIGIN:** Everyone knows that all the greatest muscle cars come from the US of A. America was the nation that invented the muscle car, and it still makes the lairiest, scariest examples on the planet. However, Australia makes a few good ones, and we in Britain have been known to cook up a fine muscle car on occasion…

**NOISE:** A muscle car must make a noise like an elephant trapped in a small wardrobe. Forget about the pleasant, dulcet tones of a Ferrari or an Aston Martin – muscle cars make a deafening racket and they don't care who hears it.

**Top Gear's top five modern muscle cars**
Dodge Challenger: **THUNDEROUS!**
Ford Mustang: **NOISY!**
Chevrolet Camaro: **RAUCOUS!**
Cadillac CTS-V coupe: **ROWDY!**
Vauxhall VXR8: **SHOUTY!**

**INTERIOR:** No super-soft yak leather or walnut dashboard here. Muscle car cabins are basic, simple affairs with nothing to distract you from the basic, simple act of driving in a straight line.

**DRIVER:** Big, noisy muscle cars tend to be driven by big, noisy American people usually called 'Bubba' or 'Chuck'. Either that, or 'Richard Hammond', who isn't big or American. In fact, one of the surest signs that you're following a muscle car is if Richard's behind the wheel.

**ON THE STEREO:** The only music to listen to when driving a muscle car is classic American rock. Bruce Springsteen is the perfect choice. If you haven't heard of him, ask your parents. Listening to classical music, hip-hop or Scandinavian nose-harp in a muscle car is just wrong.

**TYRES:** Muscle cars MUST be rear-wheel drive. What's more, a muscle car must be able to light up its rear tyres until you can't see the car for all the smoke. It's the only polite way to leave the supermarket car park…

**DOORS:** Some people will claim that muscle cars must only have two doors. This is not true. Muscle cars can be two- or four-door, but – and this is very, very important – they can't be hatchbacks. Sticking a huge engine in your parents' Ford Focus won't turn it into a muscle car. You'll probably get in a lot of trouble too.

**HANDLING:** Not really. Muscle cars are very good at one thing: going seriously fast in a straight line. However, because America was built without any corners, they're not so good when it comes to getting round bends.

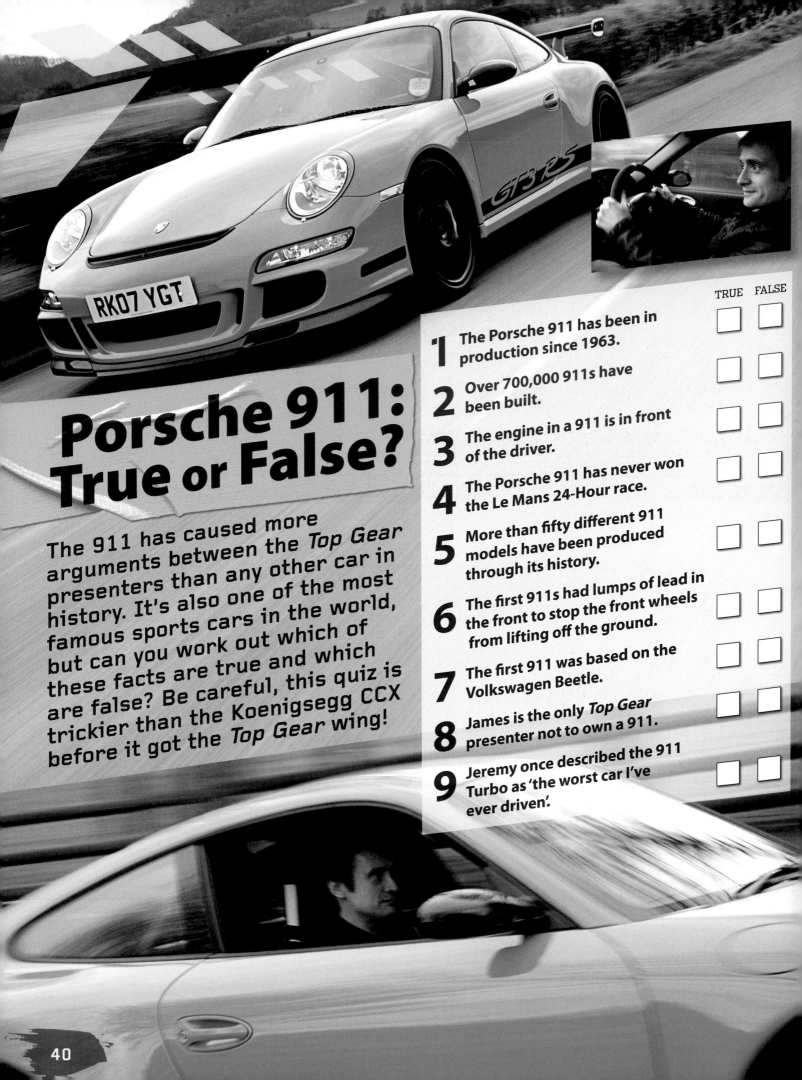

# Porsche 911: True or False?

The 911 has caused more arguments between the *Top Gear* presenters than any other car in history. It's also one of the most famous sports cars in the world, but can you work out which of these facts are true and which are false? Be careful, this quiz is trickier than the Koenigsegg CCX before it got the *Top Gear* wing!

|  |  | TRUE | FALSE |
|---|---|---|---|
| **1** | The Porsche 911 has been in production since 1963. | ☐ | ☐ |
| **2** | Over 700,000 911s have been built. | ☐ | ☐ |
| **3** | The engine in a 911 is in front of the driver. | ☐ | ☐ |
| **4** | The Porsche 911 has never won the Le Mans 24-Hour race. | ☐ | ☐ |
| **5** | More than fifty different 911 models have been produced through its history. | ☐ | ☐ |
| **6** | The first 911s had lumps of lead in the front to stop the front wheels from lifting off the ground. | ☐ | ☐ |
| **7** | The first 911 was based on the Volkswagen Beetle. | ☐ | ☐ |
| **8** | James is the only *Top Gear* presenter not to own a 911. | ☐ | ☐ |
| **9** | Jeremy once described the 911 Turbo as 'the worst car I've ever driven'. | ☐ | ☐ |

# How to Drive Up a Volcano

If you're stupid enough to drive to the mouth of a volcano, you need to take some precautions. Here's how to do it the *Top Gear* way...

We're on **fire**. Right, I'm off!

**Step 1:** Take one Toyota Hilux pick-up truck.

**Step 2:** Bolt a sheet of corrugated iron to the roof. This will protect you against lumps of flying lava!

**Step 3:** Deflate your tyres. This will give you more grip and stop them exploding when they get hot!

**Step 4:** Fit a water-cooling system for the tyres. Fill an oil drum with water, and run pipes to each of the wheels. The cold water will stop your tyres setting on fire – but don't forget to add some vodka to the water to stop it freezing!

**Step 5:** Keep moving. If you stay still for too long, your tyres will catch fire.

**Step 6:** Don't get too close. Volcanoes boil away at temperatures well over 1000°C. That's hot enough to vaporise a pick-up… and you!

**Step 7:** Need to collect some magma to take home? Remember to bring your collecting equipment: a trowel on a pole, and a metal bucket…

# THE FASTEST CARS... EVER!

In 2010, with James May on test-driving duties at Volkswagen's test track, Bugatti's 1200bhp Veyron Super Sport became the fastest production car ever. Here are the cars that used to hold the record...

## 268mph

### 2010: Bugatti Veyron Super Sport

Bugatti wasn't impressed at losing its speed record to the Americans. But instead of giving up and walking away, they came back with a faster, even-more-powerful Veyron…

## 256mph

### 2007: SSC Ultimate Aero TT

If you've never heard of Shelby SuperCars, you're not alone. The tiny American company was almost unknown until it smashed the Veyron's record in 2007 on a closed road in Washington.

## 253mph

### 2005: Bugatti Veyron

The Veyron has broken dozens of records, but this might be the biggest of the bunch. It was the first car in history capable of 250mph… and probably the only car ever capable of beating a plane from Italy to London!

**240mph**

### 2005: Koenigsegg CCR
The CCR is the predecessor to the car that tried to kill the Stig by flinging him into a tyre barrier. Taking it to 240mph required superhuman braveness – but the CCR didn't even hold the record for a full year!

**231mph**

### 1994: McLaren F1
McLaren's amazing three-seater held the speed record for over a decade, and is still recognised as perhaps the greatest supercar of all time. As Richard discovered in Abu Dhabi, it'll still push the Veyron very, very close!

### 1993: Jaguar XJ220
BBC Formula One commentator and racing driver Martin Brundle took the speed record to Britain when he charged the way to 213mph on a high-speed bowl in Italy. On the straight, Jaguar reckons the XJ220 could have done 220mph!

**213mph**

# MAKE MAY'S SHIRT

James wears a wide variety of... interesting shirts. Can you design something that he'd like?

# Odd Cee'd Out

Each of these pictures of the boring Kia Cee'd has a matching pair — except one. Which is the odd Cee'd out?

45

# The Middle East Challenge

Can the boys make it from a scary airbase in northern Iraq all the way to Bethlehem without running into one of the MANY hazards?

## START

**IRAQ Disaster!** Your car has blown up, smoke pouring from under the bonnet. Switch into the back-up Astra and head back to the start.

**IRAQ Roadblock!** You've been stopped by the police for looking suspiciously foreign. Back to the start for you…

**IRAQ Slippery road!** You've taken a nasty spin and bent your car. Head back to the start and get it repaired.

**TURKISH BORDER** The locals have found your novelty bullet lighter, and they think it's real. They're not letting you in. Back to the start.

**IRANIAN BORDER Oh no!** For political reasons, the BBC isn't allowed into Iran. Ant and Dec could cross the border, but you can't. Go back to the start.

**SOUTH TURKEY** You've been caught driving at night in dangerous territory! The authorities have sent you back to the start.

**TURKEY** One of your sparkplugs has popped out. Get it repaired and start again.

**SYRIAN BORDER Eh?** Your idiot colleagues have rewired your stereo to play Genesis on full blast. Fix your electrics and head back to the start.

**SYRIA The locals have seen through your disguise!** There's no way you'll get over the Israeli border now. Head back to the start and give it another go.

**SYRIA** Yuck! You've been bitten by a nasty insect and your arm has swollen up like a balloon. Get to the doctor, then return to the start.

**SYRIAN DESERT** You've got trapped in a desert trench. Repair your battered car and head back to the beginning.

**SYRIAN DESERT** Your foolish colleagues have knocked you out with a tow rope. Off to hospital, and then back to the start.

**SYRIAN DESERT** You've knocked your radiator out on a bump. Bolt it back in and return to the start.

**JORDAN** Smash! You've had a collision during an 'Old Testament NASCAR' race. Repair your missing bumper and go back to the beginning.

**SYRIA** You've got a flat tyre. Grab your space-saver spare and have another go from the start.

**ISRAEL BORDER Disaster!** The Israeli guards have discovered that you visited Syria. They're not letting you in.

**ISRAEL** You've fallen into the Sea of Galilee. Drenched, you're off back to the start. Sorry.

**ISRAEL Where's the toilet?** You've encountered some… stomach problems. So close to the finish, but head back to the start.

**BETHLEHEM You made it!** Collect Baby Stig and return to the *Top Gear* test track…

# FINISH

# DOCTOR, DOCTOR!

The doctor's surgery was a busy place on the boys' big Middle East road trip. Here are the doctor's notes from the trip, but they've become separated from the photos of the patients. Can you match them up?

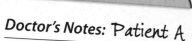

### Doctor's Notes: Patient A

Patient arrived with a sore head, mumbling nonsense about 'hydraulic lash adjusters' and 'starter ring gears'. Patient seemed unsure of where he was, repeatedly getting lost and seeming unable to understand simple directions. Upon being discharged, the patient seemed incapable of driving at more than 10mph.

### Doctor's Notes: Patient B

Patient arrived with a swollen arm, complaining of having suffered an insect bite. Patient was also complaining about several hundred other things, including the fact that deserts were too sandy, his car wasn't fast enough and that his travelling companions were LITERALLY THE MOST STUPID HUMANS IN THE WORLD EVER.

### Doctor's Notes: Patient C

Patient arrived clutching his stomach and asking the way to the toilet. When asked the reason for his complaint, the patient blamed it on 'weird foreign food' and 'not being able to find any nice English cornflakes for breakfast'.

# Who's Wisen?

Last Christmas, the boys were set the challenge of driving from northern Iraq to Bethlehem, re-enacting the journey of the three wise men at the time of Jesus's birth. But did they manage to match the wisdom of the ancient travellers? Er, no. Not even close...

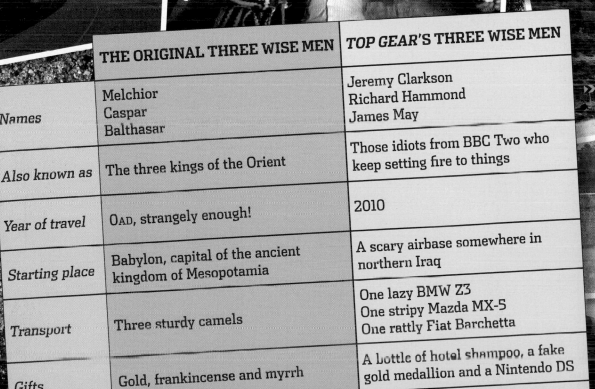

|  | THE ORIGINAL THREE WISE MEN | TOP GEAR'S THREE WISE MEN |
|---|---|---|
| Names | Melchior<br>Caspar<br>Balthasar | Jeremy Clarkson<br>Richard Hammond<br>James May |
| Also known as | The three kings of the Orient | Those idiots from BBC Two who keep setting fire to things |
| Year of travel | 0AD, strangely enough! | 2010 |
| Starting place | Babylon, capital of the ancient kingdom of Mesopotamia | A scary airbase somewhere in northern Iraq |
| Transport | Three sturdy camels | One lazy BMW Z3<br>One stripy Mazda MX-5<br>One rattly Fiat Barchetta |
| Gifts | Gold, frankincense and myrrh | A bottle of hotel shampoo, a fake gold medallion and a Nintendo DS |
| Method of navigation | Following a star | Maps with insufficient detail, guesswork, road signs |

**Lotus 2-Eleven** Though it's happiest flying round a racetrack, the mad 2-Eleven is actually legal to drive on the road. Just make sure you watch out for rain. And low-flying birds. And speed limits…

Last year, the boys were challenged to buy some budget trackday cars: vehicles that can drive you to a circuit and then thrash everything else around it. It's fair to say that they didn't choose especially wisely. If they'd been given a bit more cash, they could have bought one of these little beauties instead…

**Caterham R500** 263bhp might sound like a modest amount of power, but the R500 is so light that it'll run rings around Lamborghinis and Aston Martins. Warning: Stig-grade driving skills required.

**Mitsubishi Evo FQ400** From Monday to Friday, this four-wheel drive saloon is a sensible family car. But show it a track at the weekend and it transforms into a supercar-destroying monster!

**Ariel Atom V8** Sticking a big V8 into the tiny Atom – a car that weighs about as much as a stick insect that's been on a diet – is a ridiculous plan. That's why we like it so much.

**Caparo T1** It's a Formula One car for the road! The Caparo isn't the most reliable car ever made, but it's one of the very fastest. Probably best to have a medical team on standby, though.

**KTM X-Bow R** For years, KTM built motorbikes. This is its first shot at a car – and it's closer to a superbike than almost anything else on the road. Or track. Handle with care.

**Ferrari 430 Scuderia** Not many people thought the Ferrari F430 was too slow and too heavy. Ferrari did. That's why it cooked up this lightweight, hyperspeed special with no creature comforts at all.

**Renaultsport Clio 200 Cup** Small French hatchbacks don't generally make very good track-day cars. But the Clio 200 is fizzier than a can of pop that's been tied to a pneumatic drill for a week.

**Porsche 911 GT2 RS** Porsche's most powerful car ever will hit 205mph and devour everything else on the circuit. Its nickname is 'The Widowmaker'. It's best not to ask why…

**Subaru Impreza Cosworth** There are hot hatches… and then there's the Impreza Cosworth. With 400bhp and four-wheel drive, it'll make mincemeat of anything slower than a hypercar. And still have room for all your shopping.

# How to Beat the Aussies Fair and Square

The Australians might be our sworn enemies on the cricket pitch, but that doesn't excuse any cheating on the racetrack. Here's the *Top Gear* guide to beating the Aussies without resorting to any underhand tactics. Well, maybe just a few...

> That gag was not funny in 1938!

> It is here!

> It's upside down!

> It won't be when you get home. You watch it on TV there, it'll all be the right way up.

## 1. Arrange them a comfortable taxi

Make sure they get from the airport to the track in style by booking a luxurious limousine for the journey...

> Why do **I** have to do the first event? And why does it have to be in an old van?

*Probably full of carpet and tools. A bit rusty.*

*Six-litre V8 engine from the Corvette. Fast.*

## 3. Make them feel at home

Australians are used to being upside-down. It's your duty as a host to make them feel comfortable, no matter how much effort you have to go to...

> Where are we? I can't see! I have no reference!

## 2. Let them choose the first event

STEVE: 'This is a working man's one-kilometre drag race. We'll put a typical Aussie commercial vehicle against a typical Pommie commercial vehicle to see which is the fastest...'

> What is that? It says JAGUAR! And it's TURBOCHARGED?

> What is this thing? It's **insane!**

> Did you say we **weren't** allowed to bring a Jaguar-propelled van? No.

# The Best Car in the World?

> It's full of **exciting** buttons that do **many** things.

> Cheaper than a Vauxhall Astra!

> James thought Jeremy was mad when he declared the Skoda Yeti to be better than any other car. So Jezza set out to prove it.

> How does it look?

> Honestly? Not brilliant.

*More headroom than a Ford Focus!*

*Tough enough to cope with a small dog\**

*Smoother than a Range Rover when getting a tattoo!*

*Seats more people than a Maybach!*

*Tough enough to cope with the Fire Brigade!*

*Room for Sienna Miller in the glovebox!*

*Faster round Donington than a Ferrari 308 GTS!*

> Oh that's impressive. Ooh yes.

*Comes with ABS, EDC, EDD, ASR, EVL, DSR, ESBS and HBA!*

*Better aircon than a Rolls-Royce!*

\*Not much of a test, really

Ladies and gentlemen, I give you the Skoda Yeti. With a **helicopter** on the roof.

And strong enough to park on top!

### Yeti Challenge!

Use the helipad above as a template to create your own and stick it on top of a remote control car. How many objects can you pile on top of it without them all toppling off?

# The Mighty Atom

Take a rollerskate, and strap a rocket on it. That's the basic principle behind the new Ariel Atom V8. James loved it — but just how good is it?

> What happens when you take a **very** light car and put a **very** big engine in it?

> It's as **crisp** as a bag of crisps!

> Driving the V8 Atom is one of the **great** driving experiences of my life!

## Ariel Atom V8

- Engine: 3 litre V8
- Power: 500bhp
- 0-60mph: about 2.5s
- Top speed: 170mph
- Price: £150,000

### Pluses

- Power-to-weight ratio of over 900hp/tonne – twice as good as the Veyron or Enzo
- The addition of a tiny plastic windscreen stops your face from going all flabby and ruined, like Jeremy's

### Minuses

- No extras. Nothing. No radio, glovebox, central locking, doors, roof, spare wheel, boot, cupholders, GPS, cruise control, towbar…
- Costs waaaay more than the standard Atom, which was already pretty excellent
- They're only making twenty-five of them, and most are already sold

0–100–0mph versus a Lexus LF3 and a Lamborghini Gallardo: WINNER!

One lap of the TG track against a BMW S1000 RR superbike: WINNER!

One lap of the TG track in the hands of the Stig: NEW LAP RECORD!

| ARIEL ATOM V8 | 1.15.1 |
| BUGATTI VEYRON S.S | 1.16.8 |
| GUMPERT | 1.17.1 |
| ASCARI A10 | 1.17.3 |

Richard was determined to win a race between a Porsche and a Beetle powered by nothing but gravity.

**That** is a wretched, awful miserable, spluttering, puttering, slow, noisy, ugly piece of hateful misery and the worst attempt at a people's car the world has ever suffered, **but**...

...from it evolved **this**, the acknowledged finest driver's car and ultimate automotive precision tool that mankind has **ever** created.

This really should be **very close** indeed.

On your marks... get set...

GO!

God, I lost! **No!** Not the Beetle! Well that's – my life is **over.**

CRRUMMP

## Some other things *Top Gear* has dropped

- A caravan
- Various cars, while trying to hit a different caravan
- A stopwatch
- A piano
- Another piano
- Yet another piano
- Part of Richard's roof, in France
- Jeremy's motorhome, in Cornwall
- A Bentley Mulsanne with James in it, in Albania

# The Lap of Luxury

If money's no object and you want a fast, luxurious saloon, *Top Gear* is here to help you make your final choice.

It's chuffing **marvellous**, this motor.

## Rolls-Royce Ghost

- Engine: 6.6 litre V12
- Power: 563bhp
- 0-60mph: 4.7s
- Top speed: 155mph
- Price: £200,000

## Mercedes S65

- Engine: 6 litre V12
- Power: 603bhp
- 0-60mph: 4.4s
- Top speed: 155mph
- Price: £160,000

I have **never** experienced a car this big... and so powerful!

## Bentley Mulsanne

- Engine: 6.7 litre V8
- Power: 505bhp
- 0-60mph: 5.1s
- Top speed: 184mph
- Price: £220,000

I am **terribly** disappointed by the Bentley.

What we've got here are three cars, they were made in the same factory by the same robots, at roughly the same time, and they've all been driven in the same country by the same sort of people, so they **should** be the same. But I **bet** they're not.

# Spot the Similarities

Sent to go and buy four-seater convertibles for under £2000, the chaps each ended up with a BMW 325i. The cars were all pretty rotten, but in different ways.

*Can you spot ten differences between these pictures?*

## Page 14: Match the Simile

'It sounds like squirrels are being pushed into the engine' – **Prodrive P2**

'Listen to that noise! It's like Barry White eating wasps' – **Mercedes-Benz CLS 55 AMG**

'This car can be vicious, but in an amusing way, like a shark in a funny hat' – **Pagani Zonda F**

'It sounds like the god of thunder gargling with nails' – **Mercedes McLaren SLR**

'It's a bit like sliding down a black run in a wardrobe' – **Overfinch Range Rover**

'It sounds like a bear. Like a burning bear' – **Ferrari 458**

'It stops like a duck on a frozen lake' – **Hummer H2**

'It looks like a dog doing a poo' – **Chrysler Crossfire**

'It's like driving a – fast! – bouncy castle!' – **Saab 9-5 Hot Aero**

'This car is like an elephant with the reflexes of a water-boatman' – **Bentley Continental Supersports**

## Page 15: Piste bashing

The Dakkar will just win with 30 spaces, against 31 for the snowmobilers.

## Page 31: Surf's Up!

```
D U P S M I R O B E D I T H R O A X
E D A P O N I P D A R N H A N E B U
E N F L O C F L R L U D A W A V E S
W I S A N D N I A K N R C T G R A P
A Q O S W E T S H I T U K H G O C R
E N I H I F U T G C O B E O I M H I
S I V O P I I A E U P L N S N A I T
O G E F E T T M F T Y A D S E N S A
  P G S F O H R O   R T     E O R T I
  P O T E U U O R L A H D L C S R T O
  A F I N T W A E A M O K L U U J N
  Y S B A I R R X N E R U W I R R U
      C O R N W A L L O Z I S N F A C K
      N I A M O P E R R I F L U H M H L
        M L C E Z A T E M O H R O T J R A
        U E N R A N T T V E O U R O A E I W
          Y B U M X O S E E R Q N G P R E W S
            R O L S U T O I L R D E G Y L D P M S
```

## Page 33: Mixed-up F1 Drivers

SPIES A FLAME – Felipe Massa

KERB BE WARM – Mark Webber

JUST NO BONNET – Jensen Button

VALIANT BEE TESTS – Sebastian Vettel

SUCH A CLICHE HAMMER – Michael Schumacher

NOON AND LOAFERS –Fernando Alonso

SAW THE MILLION – Lewis Hamilton

## Page 40: Porsche 911 True or False?

1. TRUE: This makes it one of the oldest cars still built today.
2. TRUE: It's one of the best-selling sports cars of all time!
3. FALSE: It's in the rear of the car.
4. FALSE: It has won it twice, in 1979 and 1998.
5. TRUE
6. TRUE
7. TRUE
8. FALSE: Both James and Richard own 911s, but Jeremy doesn't.
9. FALSE: In fact, Jeremy was seriously impressed by the 911 Turbo – it's the first 911 he's ever liked!

## Page 45: Odd Cee'd Out

1.A, 2.C, 3.F, 4.E, 5.J, 6.G, 7.I, 8.H, 9.D,10.B.

Picture 11 is the odd Cee'd out.

## Page 48: Doctor, Doctor!

Patient A – James May

Patient B – Jeremy Clarkson

Patient C – Richard Hammond

## Page 59: Spot the Similarities

In picture B:

# More books from Top Gear

**A REASONABLY PRICED BOOK OF STUFF**

SOME SAY IT'S INTERESTING BUT ESSENTIALLY USELESS

ISBN: 9781405907958

**ULTIMATE** Stupidly Hard **QUIZ BOOK**

500 OF OUR TOUGHEST QUESTIONS

NOW IN ONE BUMPER BOOK!

ISBN: 9781405908283

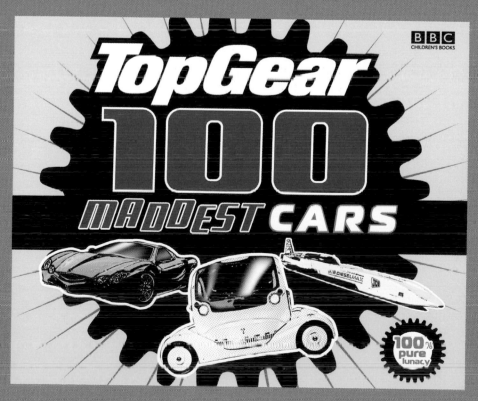

**TopGear 100 MADDEST CARS**

100% pure lunacy

ISBN: 9781405907934